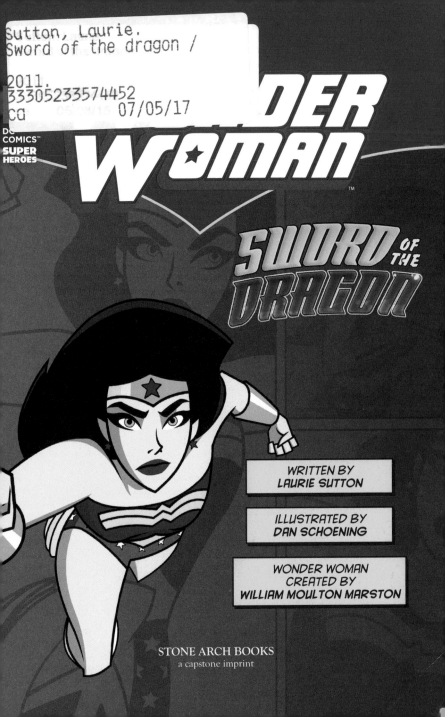

DC
COMICS™
SUPER
HEROES

WONDER WOMAN

™

SWORD OF THE DRAGON

WRITTEN BY
LAURIE SUTTON

ILLUSTRATED BY
DAN SCHOENING

WONDER WOMAN
CREATED BY
WILLIAM MOULTON MARSTON

STONE ARCH BOOKS
a capstone imprint

Published by Stone Arch Books
A Capstone Imprint
1710 Roe Crest Drive
North Mankato, Minnesota 56003
www.capstonepub.com

STAR13057

Cataloging-in-Publication Data is available at the Library of Congress
website.

ISBN: 978-1-4342-1979-4 (library binding)
ISBN: 978-1-4342-2760-7 (paperback)

Summary: While flying her jet, Wonder Woman spots a message in the
clouds, demanding that she head to the ancient monument of Stonehenge.
When she arrives, the Amazon Princess finds dozens of tourists held
hostage by Morgaine Le Fey! The sorceress threatens to harm them, if
Wonder Woman doesn't steal the Star Sword of Merlin. Believing she has
no choice, the super hero agrees, but knows her task will not be easy. She
must convince a guardian dragon that the sword will fall into the wrong
hands — if it is not in her own.

Art Director: Bob Lentz
Designer: Kay Fraser

Printed in the United States of America in Stevens Point, Wisconsin.
112013   007879R

TABLE OF CONTENTS

CHAPTER 1

TOURIST TRAP

Wonder Woman loved to fly in her Invisible Jet on bright, blue days. The plane was clear as glass and could change shapes. It could be a submarine, a motorcycle, or even a spaceship. But, no matter what it looked like, it was ultra fast.

Wonder Woman could see the clouds around her feet. She looked down at the white, fluffy shapes. Suddenly, Wonder Woman gasped in surprise. The clouds were moving in a strange way. They were forming words!

"Attention, Wonder Woman!" she read out loud. It was a message for her! "Come to Stonehenge in England — or else the hostages are doomed!"

She did not know who had made this threat. She did not know who had the power to move those clouds. All she needed to know was that people were in danger, and they needed her help.

Wonder Woman immediately turned her Invisible Jet toward England.

Wonder Woman flew over the Atlantic Ocean at super-speed and reached England in no time. Very soon she circled over Stonehenge — a large ring of giant stones built a long time ago. Stonehenge was so old that nobody knew who had built it.

A woman stood in the middle of the stone ring. There was something strange about her. She glowed! Wonder Woman flew lower. Now she saw people tied to the stones. They glowed, too!

"That group of tourists needs my help," Wonder Woman said to herself.

Wonder Woman landed her jet and then jumped to the ground. She walked over to the glowing woman, who looked familiar.

"I know you!" Wonder Woman said. "You're Morgaine Le Fey."

The woman laughed an evil laugh. She was a sorceress from King Arthur's time. Merlin and the Knights of the Round Table had been her enemies long ago.

"I saw your message," Wonder Woman said. "What do you want?"

"I want you to steal the Star Sword of Merlin," Morgaine said. She pointed at the tourists. "If you don't, I'll turn my new friends here into hideous monsters!"

Wonder Woman frowned. It was against the Amazon code to steal. But if she did not do what Morgaine demanded, these people were doomed.

The sorceress saw Wonder Woman pause. "I mean what I say!" Morgaine said.

She waved her arms in a sharp motion. **ZZZAPPPPPPP!** Streaks of energy and light flashed from her fingers. "Frog and worm! Webs and wings! Transform!"

Morgaine pointed at one of the trapped tourists. The man's arms turned into wings. His feet grew webbing like a duck. He tried to yell, but his voice croaked.

"Who will be next?" Morgaine taunted.

"Stop!" Wonder Woman said. "I will get the sword, but only to save these people."

"I knew you would see things my way," Morgaine said, laughing.

"Why don't you get the sword yourself?" Wonder Woman asked.

"Because it pleases me to command the great Amazon Princess," Morgaine sneered.

Morgaine stepped forward. "You have powers granted by the gods," she said. "Gaea gave you strength. Hermes gave you speed. You have the wisdom of Athena. But now, I have power over you!"

Wonder Woman knew Morgaine was hiding something. There was a reason why the sorceress couldn't get the sword herself. Otherwise she would have done it already.

"The sword is in Merlin's Cave at Tintagel Castle," Morgaine said. "Oh, and one last thing."

"What is that?" Wonder Woman asked, curious.

"The sword is guarded by a dragon!" Morgaine replied, laughing.

"I hope your Amazon powers will protect you, Wonder Woman!" Morgaine taunted.

All of a sudden Wonder Woman understood why Morgaine needed her to steal the magic weapon.

"I know the reason you can't steal the sword," Wonder Woman said. "Your magic doesn't work in Merlin's Cave. He's more powerful than you."

Morgaine was full of anger at Wonder Woman for guessing the truth.

"You're wasting your time," the evil sorceress said. "Now go, before I turn the rest of these humans into geese!"

Wonder Woman jumped into her Invisible Jet and flew to Tintagel Castle.

Tintagel was not far from Stonehenge. It took Wonder Woman only a few minutes to reach the castle in her jet. Tintagel was the birthplace of King Arthur and was built on a cliff by the sea. There was not much left after all these centuries. The stone walls had crumbled into ruins.

Wonder Woman flew around and around the castle. There was no sign of a cave entrance anywhere.

If the cave is not on land, then it has to be under the water, the Amazon Princess thought.

"Invisible Jet," Wonder Woman said. "Transform into a submarine!"

At once, the jet's wings pulled back into its body. A propeller grew in place of its tail. The plane slowed down and dived into the water like a seagull.

CHAPTER 2

THE MAGIC CAVE

A short time later, Wonder Woman found the cave entrance. It was a big, black hole in the cliff. As Wonder Woman guided the invisible sub, she could see letters carved in the rock. The message was written in a language as old as Merlin. It read, "BEWARE! MONSTERS PROTECT THIS PLACE! DO NOT ENTER!"

"Monsters, too?" Wonder Woman said. "Morgaine left out that little detail."

As the sub entered the cave, a giant sea serpent suddenly appeared in its path.

Then bright flashes lit up the cave, but it wasn't lightning. When the serpent opened its mouth, Wonder Woman saw that it had electricity for teeth!

"You're not making a meal out of me!" Wonder Woman shouted at the monster.

She drove the sub this way and that way and up and down. The sea serpent chased her as fast as it could go. Every time it took a bite at the sub, sparks flew like fireworks.

The monster tried its best to catch Wonder Woman, but she was too fast. The sub escaped down a tunnel that was too small for the creature to follow. The tunnel led upward and opened into a giant cavern. Wonder Woman surfaced and climbed out of the sub.

A faint light glowed from some writing carved into the rock above a door, which read, "TURN BACK! TROLL TERRITORY! DANGER!"

"I can't turn back now," Wonder Woman said to herself.

She took hold of the metal ring on the door and pulled. The door wouldn't budge.

"Gaea, give me strength!" Wonder Woman said, calling on the goddess of the earth. Then she pulled on the ring again, and the door came off its hinges.

Beyond the broken door was another cave. This one was full of light. It also smelled horrible. Wonder Woman held her nose and stepped inside.

Lumpy, greenish rocks covered the floor, and a warm light came from the center of the cave. Wonder Woman stepped closer to get a better look.

Suddenly one of the rocks moved. They weren't rocks at all! They were trolls gathered around a campfire. Now Wonder Woman knew why the cave smelled so bad.

"Intruder!" a troll shouted.

All of the trolls stood up. Their capes were covered with moss and mold. Wonder Woman saw that their clothing was not the only thing that made them look like rocks. Their skin was gray as granite, and their eyes were black as coal. They raised weapons made of sharp stone.

"I mean no harm," said the super hero.

The trolls did not listen to her. "Intruder! Intruder! Intruder!" they chanted.

They circled Wonder Woman. One of the trolls jabbed his spear at her. In a flash, she blocked it with one of her silver Amazon bracelets. *Zing!* Another troll lunged at her with a sharp stone knife. She blocked it with the other bracelet.

Sparks flew everywhere.

The trolls paused. This intruder was not what they expected. Their confusion did not last long. The trolls rushed toward Wonder Woman all at once.

Wonder Woman moved with the speed of Hermes. Her bracelets blocked the trolls' weapons every time. **CLINK CLANK!**

At home on Paradise Island, this would have been a game for the Amazon Princess. However, here the situation meant life or death.

Wonder Woman did not want to fight the trolls. She knew they were only trying to protect the Sword of Merlin. There was only one thing she could do.

Wonder Woman began to spin, twirling on her toes like a ballet dancer.

Wonder Woman twirled faster and faster. She was like a tornado! Soon, the trolls were sucked up into the air, swirling all around the cave.

Suddenly, Wonder Woman stopped, and the trolls crashed to the ground.

The trolls were knocked unconscious from the fall.

Wonder Woman ran toward the opening that led out of the cave. There was no writing above this one, and there was no time to wonder why. Wonder Woman quickly stepped into the dark.

CHAPTER 3

MERLIN'S MAZE

The tunnel was so dark that Wonder Woman could not see anything. Her hands and feet were invisible to her. The goddess Artemis had given Wonder Woman keen sight, but that did not help her here. She had to trust her other senses and keep moving forward.

Wonder Woman reached out on both sides and touched the rock. The walls were very close. They were also very slimy. She slid her hands up the walls until she could feel the low ceiling.

"This tunnel is a tight squeeze!" she said.

There was a weird smell, too. Wonder Woman sniffed the air but could not decide what it was — at least it was not the smell of trolls. Still, it was strangely familiar.

Something smells awful, she thought. *Like rotten eggs.*

Wonder Woman listened very carefully. She heard little chirps and squeaks. They were all over the place. The sounds moved when Wonder Woman did.

"Rats!" she said. "Or worse."

Wonder Woman walked cautiously through the dark. The rock was slippery, and the sounds and smells followed her. Suddenly, the tunnel branched off in two new directions. Right away, Wonder Woman knew what she faced.

"This is a maze," she said. "I could get lost and never find my way out."

Wonder Woman knew there was only one person in history who had beaten this kind of trap. She remembered the story of Theseus and the Minotaur. Theseus used a ball of string to trace his way through the maze and then followed it back out. Wonder Woman did not have any string, but she did have her Golden Lasso of Truth.

Wonder Woman tied one end of the lasso to a rock and entered the maze.

It was hard to know which way to go. She turned left, then right, and then left again. There were a lot of dead ends. She had to turn back and retrace her steps many times. All the twists and turns were enough to make a normal person dizzy.

The dark tunnel, the slick rock, and the invisible creatures were not the only dangers in the maze. CLICK! CLICK! CLICK! Wonder Woman heard the sound of insect legs scratching on the rock. Very *large* insect legs!

"You may not pass!" a voice suddenly said.

Wonder Woman was surprised. Insects did not speak — unless they were magic insects.

"Who are you?" she asked the darkness.

"I am the guardian of Merlin's Maze," the voice replied.

"I do not want to fight you," Wonder Woman said.

"Then turn back," the voice told her.

Wonder Woman knew that could not happen. Morgaine Le Fey was holding hostages. There was no easy way out of this situation.

"I'm coming through," Wonder Woman told the unseen insect.

"Then prepare to meet your doom!" the voice boomed.

Something went **WHOOOOSH!** over Wonder Woman's head. She felt a rush of air pass by her.

Wonder Woman quickly dodged the object. She hit the rock wall in the narrow tunnel, and that was when she realized something. A big creature wouldn't be able to fit in the small tunnel. So the creature was not big at all. Her fear came from being in the dark.

Wonder Woman knew how to get a look at the creature. She clapped her Amazon bracelets together. Sparks flew. **FLASH!** Now she saw what was in front of her!

It was not the Minotaur from the myth, but it was close. The Minotaur was half human and half bull. This creature was half human and half scorpion. Its human eyes did not like the light.

CLANK! FLASH! Wonder Woman hit her bracelets again and made more sparks. The beast scurried into the dark.

At last Wonder Woman saw a gleam of light up ahead.

"That must be the light at the end of the tunnel," she said. She held onto her Lasso of Truth and started to run toward it.

Wonder Woman burst out of the maze.

She found herself in a cave that was as bright as day.

"Who dares to enter here?" a voice boomed. It did not sound happy.

Wonder Woman looked up — and up, and up! She had reached the dragon's lair.

CHAPTER 4

THE DRAGON'S LAIR

The dragon had golden scales and eyes the color of rubies. Its teeth were as long as Wonder Woman's arms, and so were its claws. It sat on a huge heap of treasure in the middle of the cave.

"Who enters my lair?" the dragon bellowed.

"I am called Wonder Woman," she answered.

The dragon tilted its giant head down to stare at Wonder Woman.

Its red eyes glowed. "You have come to take the Star Sword of Merlin," it said.

Wonder Woman was a little surprised. The dragon had the power to detect the truth in others, just like her Lasso of Truth.

"Yes, I have," Wonder Woman said. "But it is not for me."

"You cannot have it!" the dragon roared. "I have spent centuries guarding it, all alone, in this cave. My effort will not be wasted!" THWOOOOMMMMMM!!

The dragon let loose with a stream of flame from its mouth. Wonder Woman jumped out of the way. She landed in a deep pile of golden coins.

The dragon spit more fire. Wonder Woman picked up a golden shield from the treasure hoard and blocked the flames.

When the dragon stopped to take another breath, Wonder Woman threw the shield at the beast. **CLANK!** It struck the dragon on the head.

"It's going to take more than that to defeat me," the dragon bellowed.

"Yes, it is," Wonder Woman agreed. "Try this on for size."

Wonder Woman started to throw treasure at the dragon. First it was just a few coins. Wonder Woman threw them as fast as bullets. Then she threw larger treasures. Golden goblets. Silver platters. Tables. Chairs. Suits of armor. There were a lot of things to use as weapons. Everything came at the dragon as fast as meteors.

"You are a pesky human," the dragon said, unimpressed.

The dragon took a deep breath to shoot more flame.

Wonder Woman made a giant leap and grabbed the dragon around its neck. Then she used her super-strength to flip the creature onto its back. **SLAM!**

"Ow!" the dragon exclaimed. All the breath went out of the dragon's lungs, and so did all the fire.

But fire breath was not the dragon's only weapon. It snapped its tail at Wonder Woman. **THWACK!** She went flying across the cave. Wonder Woman slammed hard against the wall.

The warrior princess got to her feet at the same time as the dragon. The dragon charged at Wonder Woman, and she charged toward the dragon.

WHAM! They smashed into each other with a huge crash! The dragon snapped its jaws at her. Wonder Woman dodged and grabbed the creature by the tail. She swung its whole body around in circles. Then she let go, and the dragon smacked against the wall. **CRAAAAACK!**

Wonder Woman quickly grabbed her Lasso of Truth. She made a noose and tossed it over the dragon's head. As soon as the lasso was around its neck, the dragon became very still. Wonder Woman was in control now.

"Show me the Star Sword," she ordered the dragon.

The dragon reached out with its claws and dug at the heap of treasure. It picked up a silvery sword. Wonder Woman gently took the weapon from the dragon.

Wonder Woman was very surprised when the dragon started to cry.

Wonder Woman had the Star Sword of Merlin in her hands. Now she could save the tourists at Stonehenge. Still, the weeping dragon made her pause. This was very strange. She felt bad for the creature.

"Are you wounded?" she asked the dragon.

"I failed my mission," the dragon replied with a sniff. "I guarded that sword for two thousand long years. I've dedicated my entire life to protecting it — and now you've taken it!"

Wonder Woman understood how the dragon felt. "I know what it's like to have a mission," she said. "But I have no choice in this matter."

"I need the sword to save people," Wonder Woman added. "Morgaine Le Fey forced me to steal it."

"Morgaine!" the dragon hissed. "I know her. She is Master Merlin's worst enemy."

"And right now, she's my worst enemy, too," Wonder Woman said.

The dragon stopped crying. Suddenly, it smiled. Its sharp teeth glittered like knives.

"Maybe we can help each other," the dragon said, slyly.

CHAPTER 5

STAR POWER

A short time later, Wonder Woman left the dragon's lair with the Star Sword. When she retraced her steps, the trolls did not attack her. When she drove the sub past the electric sea serpent, it swam away. The sword protected her. Now Wonder Woman knew why Morgaine wanted the Star Sword. It had great power.

Wonder Woman flew back toward Stonehenge. Morgaine Le Fey was busy turning tourists into weird creatures. "Well, it's about time you got back!" she said.

"I was getting bored playing with my captive audience," Morgaine said, smiling.

"I brought the Star Sword, as you requested," Wonder Woman said. "Now turn those hostages back into humans, and let them go!"

"You don't like my handiwork?" Morgaine pouted. "Oh, very well."

The sorceress waved her hands. Bright energy bolts flew toward the hostages. In a flash, all the people returned to normal.

"Now, give me the Star Sword!" the sorceress demanded.

Wonder Woman handed the weapon to Morgaine. "Foolish Amazon!" the sorceress said. "This sword gives me ultimate power!"

Morgaine swung the sword at Wonder Woman.

KKLLAAAANG! The blade hit the silver bracelets but made no mark on the metal. The sorceress looked surprised.

"Magic bracelets —?" Morgaine began.

"They were forged by Hephaestus," Wonder Woman replied. "But they are *not* magic."

Morgaine swung the sword at Wonder Woman again. **TWANNNGG!** The blade bounced off the bracelets.

"The Star Sword is supposed to cut through anything!" Morgaine shouted.

The evil sorceress paused. She did not know what to do. In an instant, Wonder Woman used her super-speed to snatch the sword from Morgaine's hands.

"The Sword is powerless," Wonder Woman said. "Unless you have the Star."

Wonder Woman reached into her belt and pulled out a sparkling gem. She placed it into the hilt of the sword. Suddenly, the blade began to glow.

"*Now* it can cut through anything," Wonder Woman said. She pointed the tip of the sword at Morgaine.

The sorceress held up her hands in surrender. She was afraid of the power of the Star Sword — just as the trolls and the sea serpent had been. Wonder Woman bound Morgaine with the Lasso of Truth. Then she used the sword to cut the magic ropes holding the hostages.

"Thank you, Wonder Woman!" they all exclaimed.

Not long afterward, Wonder Woman returned to the dragon's lair.

"The sword belongs with you," Wonder Woman told the dragon, handing it over.

The dragon smiled. It took the sword and returned it to the treasure trove.

"Thank you for telling me the secret about the Star Gem," Wonder Woman said. "It helped me defeat Morgaine Le Fey."

The dragon smiled a toothy smile. "I was glad to help the enemy of my enemy," it said.

"The enemy of my enemy is my friend," Wonder Woman said. "That's a very old saying."

"I'm a very old dragon," said the creature. "But I'm always happy to make new friends."

"Well, friend, do you have a name?" Wonder Woman asked.

"My name is Goldtalon Thunderspike Sky Amber Astra Smokewyrm the Sixth," the dragon replied.

Wonder Woman tried to say the dragon's full name, but couldn't. Even with her talent for languages, it was hard.

"You can call me Goldie, if you like," the dragon offered.

"Goldie is a good name," she said. "I know you're lonely living down here all by yourself. If you like, I could come visit you from time to time."

The dragon was very pleased. Its smile grew large, baring every fang.

"I would like that very much, Wonder Woman!" the creature said.

The dragon dug around in the piles of treasure and found a giant golden throne.

The throne was covered with jewels and precious stones. The creature set it down in front of Wonder Woman.

"How's this?" the dragon asked. "Fit for an Amazon Princess!"

Wonder Woman held back a laugh. The throne was very showy, but it was the thought that counted.

"You know what, Goldie?" Wonder Woman said. "We should go out flying together sometime."

"Flying?" the dragon exclaimed. "I haven't done that in centuries!"

FILE NO. 3765 >>> MORGAINE LE FEY

ENEMY » | ALLY | FRIEND

BIRTHPLACE: Morgaine Le Fey

OCCUPATION: Sorceress

HEIGHT: 5' 10" **WEIGHT:** 156 lbs

EYES: Blue   **HAIR:** Black

POWERS/ABILITIES: A deadly sorceress, able to teleport, read minds, shoot energy bolts from her fingertips, and harness magic.

BIOGRAPHY

As the half-sister of the medieval ruler King Arthur, Morgaine Le Fey has lived for hundreds of years. The evil sorceress maintains her immortality with powerful black magic, but her beauty could not be saved. To hide her old, withering body, Le Fey wears a suit of golden armor. However, she is not satisfied. She'll stop at nothing to regain her looks, stealing youthful energy from humans and super heroes.

LIFE-DRAINER

As Morgaine Le Fey continues to age, the body beneath her golden armor weakens. To survive, and one day regain her youthful appearance, the evil sorceress must drain life from others. Believing Wonder Woman possessed immortal energy, Le Fey once attempted to rob the Amazon Princess of her life force. However, Wonder Woman had given up her immortality upon leaving the island of Themyscira. When the sorceress attacked the super hero, Le Fey's evil plan backfired, and she turned to dust. Unfortunately, she soon returned, seeking revenge.

BLACK MAGIC

Using black magic, also known as dark arts, Morgaine Le Fey has mastered powerful skills:

Telepathy (tuh-LEH-puh-thee) — the ability to communicate using the mind alone

Telekinesis (teh-lih-kuh-NEE-sis) — the ability to move objects from one place to another without touching them, using only the mind

Teleportation (tel-uh-por-TAY-shuhn) — the act of transporting an object or person from one location or time to another, using the mind

BIOGRAPHIES

Laurie Sutton has read comics since she was a kid. She grew up to become an editor for Marvel, DC Comics, Starblaze, and Tekno Comics. She has written *Adam Strange* for DC, *Star Trek: Voyager* for Marvel, plus *Star Trek: Deep Space Nine* and *Witch Hunter* for Malibu Comics. There are long boxes of comics in her closet where there should be clothing and shoes. Laurie has lived all over the world, and currently resides in Florida.

Dan Schoening was born in Victoria, B.C. Canada. From an early age, Dan has had a passion for animation and comic books. Currently, Dan does freelance work in the animation and game industry and spends a lot of time with his lovely little daughter, Paige.

GLOSSARY

cavern (KAV-ern)—a large cave

granite (GRAN-it)—a hard, gray rock used in the construction of buildings

hostage (HOSS-tij)—someone taken or held prisoner as a way of demanding money or other conditions

keen (KEEN)—able to notice things easily

sorceress (SOR-sur-ess)—someone who performs magic by controlling evil spirits

surrender (suh-REN-dur)—to give up or admit that you are beaten in a fight or battle

tourist (TOOR-ist)—someone who travels and visits places for pleasure

transform (transs-FORM)—a piece of equipment that changes the voltage of an electric current

trove (TROV)—a valuable collection

unconscious (uhn-KON-shuhss)—not awake, and unable to see, feel, or think

DISCUSSION QUESTIONS

1. Wonder Woman helped Morgaine Le Fey steal the Star Sword. Do you think she made a good decision? Why or why not?

2. The Amazon Princess faced many challenges in this story. What is the toughest challenge that you have ever overcome?

WRITING PROMPTS

1. If you had a pet dragon and could fly anywhere in the world, where would you go? Write a short story about your adventure.

2. At the end of the story, Wonder Woman and Goldie the dragon become friends. Write about one of your own friends.

3. Pretend you are the author and write one more chapter for this book. How will Morgaine Le Fey be punished? Where will Wonder Woman and Goldie fly? You decide.

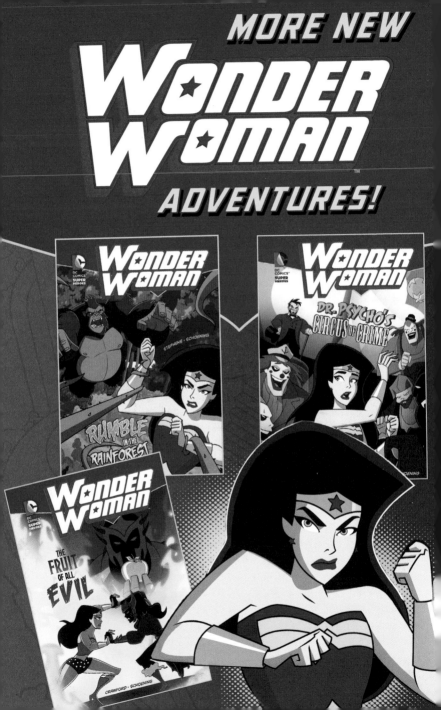

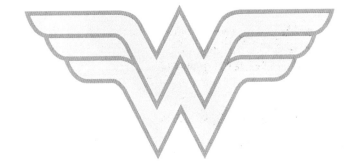